Little Badger, Terror of the Seven Seas

Written by Eve Bunting

Illustrated by LeUyen Pham

HARCOURT, INC.
San Diego   New York   London

www.harcourt.com

Library of Congress Cataloging-in-Publication Data
Bunting, Eve, 1928–
Little Badger, terror of the seven seas/written by Eve Bunting;
illustrated by LeUyen Pham.
p.   cm.
Companion to: Can you do this, Old Badger?
Summary: A young badger pretends to be a pirate until
it's time for supper.
[1. Pirates—Fiction. 2. Imagination—Fiction.
3. Badgers—Fiction.] I. Pham, LeUyen, ill. II. Title.
PZ7.B91527Li 2001
[E]—dc21   00-8451
ISBN 0-15-202395-X

First edition
H G F E D C B A

Printed in Singapore

The illustrations in this book were done in gouache
on Arches 200-pound rough press watercolor paper.
The display type was set in Elroy.
The text type was set in Galliard.
Printed and bound by Tien Wah Press, Singapore
This book was printed on totally chlorine-free
Nymolla Matte Art paper.
Production supervision by Sandra Grebenar and Ginger Boyer
Designed by Lori McThomas Buley

For
Diane
D'Andrade
—E.B.
&
L.P.

It was the time between daylight and dusk. Little Badger wobbled and waddled along the forest path.

"Little Badger, why are you walking like that?" Woodchuck asked.

"I'm a pirate," Little Badger said. "I have to wobble and waddle so I can keep my balance on the heaving deck of my pirate ship."

Woodchuck chuckled. "You are not a pirate. If you were, you would have a striped jersey and a cocked hat."

But Little Badger knew something Woodchuck didn't. Old Badger had told him. He smiled and wobble-waddled on.

"Little Badger, why are you walking like that?"
Raccoon asked.
"I'm a pirate, that's why," Little Badger said.

Raccoon tittered, and twitched his ring-tailed
tail. "You can't be a pirate. If you were, you would
have a patch over one eye."
Little Badger smiled and wobble-waddled on.

Crow swooped down from the giant oak.
"Little Badger, why are you walking like that?"
"Because I'm a pirate," Little Badger said.

Crow squinted, beady eyed. "I don't think so.
If you were a pirate, you would have a parrot—green
as grass and wild as wind—perched on your shoulder."

Little Badger smiled a little pirate smile and wobble-
waddled on.

"Little Badger, why are you walking like that?"
Chipmunk stood on his back legs.

"Because I'm a pirate, of course," Little Badger said.

Chipmunk chittered. "So where is your pirate ship? If you were a pirate, you would have a great ship with fat white sails. There'd be a skull-and-crossbones flapping from the tallest mast, and you'd be the terror of the seven seas."

"Really?" Little Badger laughed a quiet pirate *har-har-har*. He knew something Chipmunk didn't.

He knew he could be anything he wanted to be
and do anything he wanted to do as long as he used
his imagination and was home in time for supper.
Old Badger had told him.

Little Badger wobble-waddled on till he came to the clearing, where the old hollow log lay and where the bluebells were thick as bees in a honey hive.

Old Badger had come to wave good-bye.
"Steer clear of the rocks, Little Badger!"
he called.
"I will," Little Badger said. "I wish
you could come, too, Old Badger.
But pirates don't take passengers."

Then he pulled his striped jersey
over his head, cocked his cocked
hat, snapped on his eye patch,
stroked his parrot that was
green as grass and wild as wind, and stepped
aboard his pirate ship. He hoisted the fat
white sails and ran the skull-and-crossbones
up to flap from the tallest mast.

"Don't forget to be home in time for supper,
my Little Badger," Old Badger called.

"I won't forget. Good-bye,
Old Badger," Little Badger said.

And before you could say "Heave ho, me hearties!"
Little Badger sailed off across an ocean of bluebells to
be the terror of the seven seas.